Imagine...

A Million Kittens for Elmo

Featuring
Jim Henson's
Sesame Street
Muppets™

By Emily Thompson
Illustrated by Anna Randa

A SESAME STREET / GOLDEN BOOK

Published by Western Publishing Company, Inc., in conjunction with
Children's Television Workshop.

©1993 Children's Television Workshop. Jim Henson's Sesame Street Muppet Characters © 1993 Jim Henson Productions, Inc. All rights reserved. Printed in the U.S.A. No part of this book may be reproduced or copied in any form without written permission from the copyright owner. Sesame Street, the Sesame Street Sign, and Sesame Street Imagine are trademarks and service marks of Children's Television Workshop. All other trademarks are the property of Western Publishing Company, Inc. Library of Congress Catalog Card Number: 93-70346 ISBN: 0-307-13122-X/ISBN: 0-307-63122-2 (lib. bdg.) MCMXCIV

Cozy up, Daisy, and Elmo will tell you a story. Once, a long time ago, there was a king called Midas. Everything that Midas touched turned into gold. Elmo wishes Elmo had the magic touch! Imagine if everything Elmo touched turned into a kitten. . . .

One magic touch and Elmo turns a gingham dog . . .

into a calico cat! Yeah!

Two teddies turn into . . .

two tabbies! Yippee!
  Elmo could even have a million kittens!

Just think—Elmo doesn't need a magic wand to amaze even the Amazing Mumford! Elmo can use his little finger to touch the magician's rabbits and . . .

Ta-da! Kaboodles of kittens!

Elmo's kitties go everywhere Elmo goes.

Elmo wonders if Elmo's teacher likes kitties.

Ms. Carlin, look what Elmo brought for show-and-tell!

How can Elmo draw a picture
for Bert, when every crayon Elmo
touches turns into a kitty?

Maybe Elmo will give Bert a kitty instead.

How can Elmo play blocks with Ernie, when every block Elmo touches turns into a kitty?

Don't worry, kitties! Elmo will catch you!

Kitties all fall down!

After play group, we have a little snack. Thank you, Grover. Elmo is hungry.

Yipes! This ice cream cone licks back!

Poor little kitties! You're hungry, too. Come along home with Elmo.

Mommy, Mommy! Elmo is home! Could Elmo
have a little milk, please?

Could Elmo have a little *more* milk ?

Daisy, how can Elmo ever take care of all these kitties? Maybe a magic touch isn't such a good idea. Maybe Elmo doesn't need a million kittens. Maybe Elmo just needs one kitten . . .

and a million kisses instead!